GOING TO BED

by Nadine Bernard Westcott

Joy Street Books   Little, Brown and Company · Boston · Toronto

To Becky

First Edition

Library of Congress Catalog Card Number 86-28767

ISBN 0-316-93132-2

*Published simultaneously in Canada
by Little, Brown & Company (Canada) Limited*
WOR

Printed in the United States of America

Time for bed!

I put away my toys,

and hurry upstairs

to take a bath.

I put on my pajamas,
bathrobe, and slippers.

I go to the bathroom,

wash my hands, and brush my teeth.

Then I get out my clothes
for tomorrow.

Something's missing.
Now I've found it!

Mom reads my favorite book, and

Dad turns on my night-light.

Good night! Sleep tight!